Usborne
Illustrated
Stories
from
Aesop

Usborne
Illustrated Stories from Aesop

Retold by Susanna Davidson

Illustrated by
Giuliano Ferri

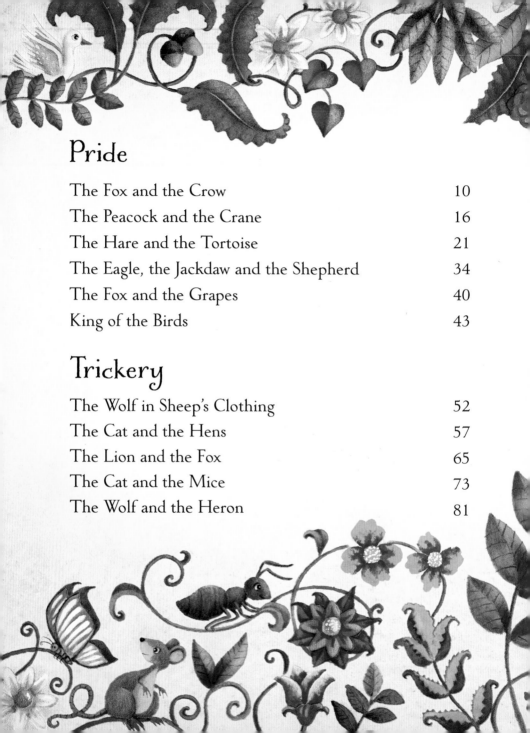

Pride

Trickery

Greed

Quarrels

Friendship

Cunning

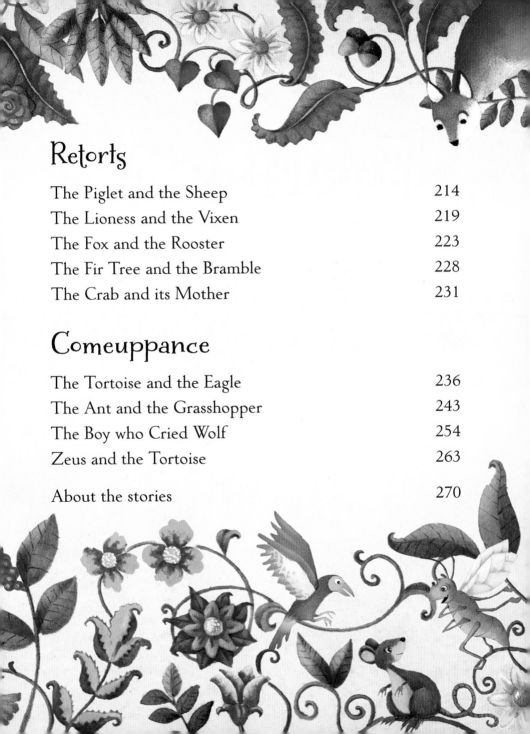

Retorts

Comeuppance

PRIDE

The Fox and the Crow

"How delicious!" thought Crow, looking at a picnic left lying in the shade. "So much food... And no one's around..."

Her beady black eye was caught by a piece of juicy meat lying just out of reach. "Oh!" thought Crow. "It's so tempting. If I swoop down fast enough," she decided, "I can get it, I'm sure."

And she went for it, darting down, a blur of black feathers. Snap, snap went her sharp beak, then she headed back into the woods, flapping her fringed wings, a very proud thief.

She couldn't resist showing off her prize, jumping up and down on her branch, brandishing the meat in front of squirrels and woodpeckers — even a woodlouse who happened to be passing by.

"My, my…" murmured Fox, glancing up from the ground. "That does look tasty." His mouth watered as he looked at the meat.

"If only I had wings," thought Fox. But he

didn't dwell on that thought for long. "After all," he told himself, "I have cunning... I can *make* it mine."

He slunk safely out of sight and sat for a while, twitching his russet red tail. Then he gave a slow smile and wandered out from the undergrowth.

"Oh Crow!" he called. "You are so beautiful, you know."

Crow looked down at Fox, cocked her head to one side, and smiled.

"So sleek! So shiny!" said Fox. "Just look at you! You're black as midnight, glossy and fine."

Crow fluffed out her feathers. She puffed out her chest.

"Your eyes sparkle like the darkest pearls," Fox went on.

Crow gazed down at herself. "I am beautiful. I *am*," she thought. "No other bird is as beautiful as me..."

Fox saw her swell with pride. He was ready now, to complete his trick.

"I've heard you have a terrible croak, though. If only you could sing, then truly you would be Queen of the Birds."

"I *should* be Queen of the Birds," thought Crow indignantly. "I can sing! And I'll prove it." She opened her glossy black beak. "Caw... Caw... Caw!" she sang.

Down, down, down fell the meat...

...right into Fox's mouth. SNAP!

He sauntered away with it, smiling. "Delicious!" he drawled, once he'd gobbled it down. "You really can't sing, can you?" he added, licking his lips. "And no queen would fall for that trick!"

Moral:
Don't fall for flattery.

The Peacock and the Crane

Peacock strutted beside the river, the blue feathers on his body as dazzling as the sun~dappled water.

Behind him, sashaying along the ground as if it had a life of its own, came his long and splendid tail.

The crane watched the peacock from the riverbed, admiring his beauty. Peacock looked back at her with scorn.

"I've never seen such knock~knees," Peacock mocked. "You must be so embarrassed. I'm surprised you don't make more effort to hide them. And as for your feathers... you poor dear! So dull!"

As he spoke, Peacock opened his tail feathers so they rose up around him like a halo. The crane was almost overcome by their beauty. The feathers shone bronze and green and blue, forming a pattern of a hundred, unblinking, iridescent eyes.

"My feathers could make a cloak fit for a princess," Peacock boasted, "a fan for an empress or a coverlet for a queen. How you must envy me! Look at your wings — so plain and white. You'll never be as beautiful as me."

Crane bowed her head. "It's true," she thought to herself. "No one gasps in pleasure as I walk by. I am nothing compared to Peacock. Nothing!"

Crane watched Peacock all day, as if by watching him, she might grow more beautiful, too. As night fell, she saw Peacock circling beneath a tree. Then, with a jump and a great flap of his wings, Peacock struggled up to roost on a low~slung branch. Crane swooped over to sit by his side.

"Why do you rest here?" she asked. "This branch is so low. Won't you be safer sleeping higher up the tree?"

"I can't fly any higher," replied Peacock

haughtily. "My tail weighs me down."

"You can't fly any higher?" repeated
Crane, sounding shocked.

"Why would I want to?" said Peacock, with
a shrug. "I'm safe enough here."

"So you've never flown up to look at the
stars?" asked Crane. "Or soared across the
sky at sunset?"

"No!" snapped Peacock. "Anyway, I don't
need to look at the stars or the sunset. If I
want to see something beautiful, all I need do
is gaze at my own reflection."

"How proud and arrogant he is," thought
Crane. She smiled. "I don't think I envy you
after all," she said. "My feathers may not

be beautiful like yours, but at least I can use them to fly."

"How dare you speak to me like that?" cried Peacock.

"I dare because for all your beauty, you're no better than a chicken in a farmyard," said Crane. "You're forever stuck on the ground, while I can soar up to the stars."

Moral:
Fine feathers don't make a fine bird.

The Hare and the Tortoise

It was a blustery March day, with a wild wind whooshing through the trees, shaking down the daffodils and scattering petals here, there and everywhere. The hare stood for a moment on the hill and then, just for the fun of it, he was off, racing across the field, thumping and leaping, as fast and as wild as the wind itself.

At the edge of the field, by a sandy path,

a group of animals stood watching as he bounded towards them.

"Oh Hare," murmured Mole, "how quickly you run."

"So swift..." cried Vole.

"So graceful," sang Squirrel.

"If only I could run as fast as you," added Mole, admiringly.

Hare puffed himself out and looked proud. "It's true," he said, frisking about on the spot, "no one is faster than me."

Someone gave a dry, raspy chuckle.

"Who dares to laugh?" snapped Hare.

Everyone turned to see Tortoise, creeping his way towards them, ancient and scaly and... slow.

"*You* could never beat me!" said Hare, his whiskers twitching in irritation.

"I could try," said Tortoise.

There was a stunned silence. Hare gasped.

"Well then, you're on," he said at last. "I'll see you here in this exact spot, next Tuesday. That should give you time to train. After all, I want to give you a chance. We'll race across the field and back."

Tortoise shook his wrinkled head. "Let's make the race longer," he suggested. "We could go through those woods, along the winding river, all the way to the great oak tree on the hill."

"Ha!" said Hare. "I'll leave you for dust. See you later, slow coach." And, with a flick of his back legs, Hare was off through the long grass, here one moment, gone the next.

The other animals looked at Tortoise pityingly.

"Poor old thing," they murmured. "What was he thinking?"

They shook their heads at him.

"Just you wait," said Tortoise, unperturbed. "Just you wait and see."

The day of the race dawned. It was sunny and warm and all the woodland animals had come out to watch, crowding around the starting line. The birds chirruped excitedly from their branches, while young rabbits and squirrels squeaked and squealed as they squeezed their way to the front to get a better view.

Tortoise waited patiently for the race to begin, but Hare couldn't help performing for the crowd. He jumped and twirled in the air, springing up and down, showing off with glee.

An owl stood before them, one wing raised in the air. "I'll start the countdown," she hooted over the commotion. "As soon as I lower my wing, the race can begin."

"Ten, nine, eight, seven, six, five, four, three, two, one…"

All the animals joined in the chant and, as Owl lowered her wing, Hare shot off in a cloud of dancing dust.

Tortoise crept forward a few paces, stopped, coughed, and crept on again.

"Come on, Tortoise!" everyone shouted, feeling sorry for him. By now, Hare was no more than a black dot in the distance, bounding away to the woods.

"I'm going to win! Ooh, yes, I'm going to win!" Hare sang to himself as he leaped along the path. The breeze rippled through his fur, and as he ran he felt at one with the woods and the wind and the song of spring, urging him on and on.

Ahead lay the winding river, and just beyond, on the brow of the hill, the great oak tree. Hare looked back through the woods, but there was no sign of Tortoise.

"This isn't really a race at all," he huffed. "Tortoise doesn't stand a chance. Where's the fun in that?"

Hare stopped running and lolloped along by the river for a while, lazily sniffing the fresh spring air, drinking in the scent of the river and the wild flowers. He yawned and stretched.

"Perhaps," thought Hare, "I should have a little nap. After all, Tortoise will be hours and hours. Then at least I can race him to the finish line."

So Hare found a soft, warm spot beside the path, closed his eyes and drifted off into a pleasant doze. And as he dozed, he dreamed... of all the races he had ever won and all the ones he was going to win.

Meanwhile, Tortoise plodded on. It was slow work, carrying his heavy shell on his back, but he kept moving his stumpy legs,

one in front of the other. By the time he left
the woods it was afternoon, the sun slipping
down behind the trees. As he made his way
along the winding river, the light began to fade.
A glorious sunset streaked across the sky.

"Come on, Tortoise!" shouted the animals at
the finishing line. "You can do it. You can win!"

Tortoise allowed himself the glimmer of a
smile, bent his head, and heaved himself up
the hill.

"We don't understand," said the moles and the voles. "Where's Hare? Whatever could have happened to him?"

"Who knows?" squeaked the mice.

"We want Tortoise to win!" added the rabbits. "Look how hard he's trying." And they squealed in excitement, urging Tortoise on.

The noise drifted down the hill to Hare's ears. They twitched. He opened his eyes, leaped up and looked around. "Oh no!" he cried. "It's nearly night. I've been asleep all this time. The race... the race..."

He set off for the finishing line, and saw, to his horror, that Tortoise was nearly there.

"NO!" cried Hare. "He can't win. This can't

be happening..."

Hare ran faster than he'd ever run in his life. Bounding up the hill, ears pinned back, he raced after Tortoise, determined to beat him, determined to win.

Slowly, slowly, Tortoise inched towards the finishing line. The air was filled with yells of, "Nearly there, Tortoise!" and "You can do it, Hare!"

"I can't believe it," tweeted the birds. "Old Tortoise might actually win."

His breath coming in great pants, Hare made leap after leap after leap. He stretched out his front paws, flattened his back and flew through the air... but he was too late.

Tortoise was already plodding slowly, but surely, over the finishing line.

There was a moment of stunned silence. Then the animals cheered and danced and crowded around Tortoise, patting him on his shell and whooping for joy.

"Who would have thought it? What a day! Tortoise beat Hare. Hooray! Hooray!"

Moral:
Slow and steady wins the race.

The Eagle, the Jackdaw and the Shepherd

Jackdaw sat in the tree, beak agape, his eyes fixed on an eagle, soaring overhead. He watched as the eagle swooped over a flock of sheep, grazing on the grassy hills, his wings glinting gold in the late summer sun. Jackdaw sighed. More than anything, he wished he could be like Eagle.

"He's so beautiful," thought Jackdaw.
"So proud and so powerful."

Then, suddenly, Eagle swept down low,
flying fast. He shot past the shepherd
on the hill, and grabbed a lamb in his
outstretched talons. The shepherd ran,
but with a triumphant cry, the eagle flew
off, the lamb dangling from his claws, and
disappeared over the distant hills.

Jackdaw watched it all longingly.

"You could never be like Eagle," came a
small voice.

Jackdaw glanced up to see a caterpillar on
the branch above, laughing at him.

"Look at your sooty black feathers," the caterpillar went on, "and your stumpy wings. What do you eat? Nuts and fruit? Baby birds? You couldn't catch anything as big as Eagle."

"I could catch you," snapped Jackdaw.

The caterpillar darted behind some leaves, then laughed.

"And I could catch a lamb," Jackdaw went on. "Ha! I could catch a ram if I wanted."

"Show me!" retorted the caterpillar, boldly popping up again.

"I will!" said Jackdaw.

He set off, flapping his scraggy black wings, cawing loudly. He made so much noise, the shepherd on the hill looked over to see what was happening.

With a dramatic dive, Jackdaw plopped down onto a ram's back and grabbed at its fleece with his claws. "Easy!" he cried.

He looked around, proud as a peacock, then flapped his wings to take off again.

Nothing happened.
The ram wouldn't budge.

"He's too... heavy," panted Jackdaw.

He bowed his head. "I'll just fly away quietly," he thought, "and pretend the whole thing never happened."

But he couldn't. He was stuck. His claws were caught in the ram's fleece, and no matter how hard he pulled and tugged... he was trapped.

From either end of the field, the shepherd and the caterpillar watched Jackdaw. They both laughed.

At last, the shepherd sauntered over to the struggling bird. He carefully placed his hands around Jackdaw's belly and untangled his claws. Then he clipped his wings, put him in his bag and that night, took him home to his children.

"What is it?" they cried. "What kind of bird is it?"

"Well, *I* think he's a jackdaw," the shepherd replied. "But *he* seems to think he's an eagle. Here," he added, holding him out. "You can have him for a pet."

Moral:
Don't try to act more important than you really are.

The Fox and the Grapes

Looking up, Fox caught sight of some grapes, high on the wall, glinting like plump purple jewels. His mouth watered. They looked full of juice, round and ripe, ready for plucking. He leaped at them, springing up on his back legs, claws outstretched. He missed.

Fox tried again, this time running and jumping, but no matter how hard he tried, the grapes stayed tantalizingly out of reach.

The hot sun beat down on his thick russet coat, and Fox began to feel tired and thirsty. And always, there were the grapes, promising to quench his thirst, taunting him with their glossy skins.

Fox began to feel angry. He looked at the grapes and snarled. They swayed slightly in the breeze. *Were they going to fall?*

No, they were not. He was never going to get them.

"I didn't want you anyway," he said, aloud.

"You're not even ripe yet," he added. "I don't need *sour* grapes."

And with that, he put his nose in the air and stalked away.

Moral:
It's easy to be rude about what you can't have.

King of the Birds

"The date's been set!" announced the finches, all of a twitter, filling the tree branches with their chatter.

"The date?" croaked Jackdaw.

"For the contest," replied the swans. "Zeus has summoned all the birds to meet on the last day of the month. He will choose the most beautiful of us all to be King of the Birds."

When that day dawned, the birds flew
down from the sky and met in the meadows
to prepare themselves for the contest. Jackdaw
was there too and, as he gazed around, his
heart sank. The other birds were dazzling.
They had long curling tail feathers, shining
crests, wings that flashed blood~red, bronze
and azure~blue...

"And what am I?" thought Jackdaw. "Black.
Plain black."

But, as the other birds began to parade
around, his eager brain was busy brewing a
plan. The ground, he realized, was littered with
feathers – brilliant and patterned as he could

never hope for his own to be. And so, while the others primped and preened, Jackdaw snatched up their fallen feathers in his sharp beak. Then he hopped behind a bush and tucked the stolen feathers between his own.

When he emerged, swaggering and triumphant, the other birds cried out. Jackdaw shone like the sun. He shimmered like a rainbow. He dazzled like the summer sea.

"Who is that?" they gasped.

Before Jackdaw could reply, Zeus drew up in his chariot and looked down at the birds. They ruffled their feathers and fanned their tails. A hundred pairs of beady black eyes pleaded, "Choose me! Choose me!"

Zeus raised his arm and pointed at Jackdaw. "This splendid creature shall be King of the Birds. He is the most beautiful by far."

Then Zeus, satisfied that his job was done, sped on his way. The other birds gawked and gasped. "Who is it?" they asked. "Who did he choose? We've never seen this bird before."

They stalked up to Jackdaw and peered at him with narrowed eyes.

"How odd!" said Peacock. "He has tail feathers just like mine."

"And those on his wing... are mine!" squawked Parrot.

"I know who it is!" cried the cockatoo. "Wicked old Jackdaw! You've stolen our feathers. And our crown!"

Jackdaw backed away.

"Let's get our feathers back!" said a furious finch.

And all at once the birds descended on Jackdaw, jabbing at him with their beaks.

"Stop!" cried Jackdaw. "Stop! Stop!"

But no one listened. And when they had finished, Jackdaw had been stripped of his stolen cloak of glory. The mangled feathers lay on the ground and Jackdaw, once again... was just a Jackdaw.

Moral:
You can't hide who you really are.

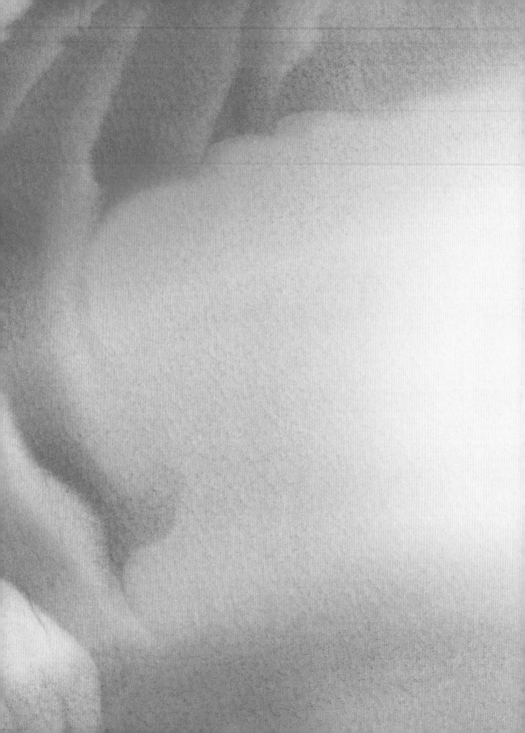

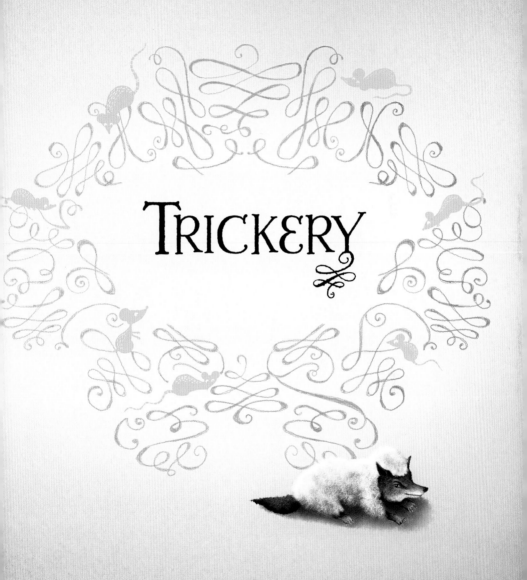

TRICKERY

The Wolf in Sheep's Clothing

As day broke, the wolf crept from his lair and followed the scent of the sheep up the hill. He made his way cautiously, moving from bush to bush for cover. When he reached the top of the hill, he was rewarded with the sight of a fat flock, grazing peacefully on the lush grass. Then he snarled as he glimpsed the shepherd standing over them, carefully scanning the view for danger.

"He's always here," growled Wolf. "If I could only think of a way to outwit him..."

Then something caught his eye — an old sheepskin, lying abandoned on the ground. The wolf waited until the shepherd had turned away, before pouncing on the skin. He grabbed it in his long yellow teeth and dragged it back to his hiding place.

"What a wonderful piece of luck," thought Wolf. "Now I know how I can get my teeth on those sheep."

He shrugged the sheepskin over his own coat and, with his head down, he slipped among the flock. His scent was covered by that of the sheepskin and to his amazed delight, his plan worked. None of the sheep noticed, nor the shepherd. But Wolf told himself to wait. Patience was the key if he were truly going to feast on the flock.

As the light began to fade, the shepherd called to the sheep and herded them down the hill, back to the safety of their pen. Wolf was with them.

The shepherd shut the gate and Wolf grinned. "He's locked me in with the sheep," he chuckled. "I can eat all night."

Wolf gave a contented sigh, knowing he wouldn't have to go far for his supper.

Listening to the peaceful bleats of the sheep, he shut his eyes, and in no time, was fast asleep.

But even before the shepherd had reached his home, he remembered he wanted some meat for his supper. So he returned to the pen, took out his knife, and killed the first sheep that came to hand. Only when he'd dragged the body out of the pen and laid it on the ground before him, did he realize it was a wolf in sheep's clothing.

"Oh ho, my old enemy," said the shepherd. "It seems your disguise worked a little too well."

Moral:
Things aren't always what they seem.

The Cat and the Hens

Cat was tired of mice. He prowled the streets, looking for something else to eat. The trouble was, birds flew away at the sight of him and frogs... yuck! Too slimy.

"You should try chickens," said his friend, the fox. "They're delicious. Juicy and tasty and so easy to catch."

"Thank you," said Cat, and he padded off to the nearest farm, following his nose.

Before long, he heard a crowing and a squawking and he knew he was close. He stretched up against a tree and carefully sharpened his claws, listening to the contented cluck of the hens.

"They sound fat and foolish," thought Cat. "I'll get them easily. No problem at all."

He flattened his ears and lowered his back, tail twitching cautiously. Then, with furtive steps, he slunk further onto the farm, eyes darting left and right, searching for the hen house.

"Curses," he hissed. A high wire fence surrounded the hens. He tried the gate — it was locked.

"This isn't as easy as I'd hoped," Cat yawned. "I think it's time I had a nap."

Beside the hen house was a leafy bush. Cat lay under it and fell fast asleep, snoring gently.

"What's that cat doing here?" clucked the hens, peering at him with their beady eyes.

"Just taking a nap," shrugged one, scratching in the dust for worms.

The other hens shook their heads. "Did you see the way he slunk into the farmyard? He's up to no good, that's for sure."

The hens watched him for a while, but the cat slept on, snoozing in the summer shade.

He was woken only by the sound of the farmer's feet, stomping past him in heavy boots. Behind the farmer came his wife, an egg basket clasped in her hands.

"Those two hens are sick," he heard the farmer say. "We should call in the vet."

"Poor old dears," said the farmer's wife. "In the meantime, I'll give them some extra hay."

Cat laughed slyly to himself. "I know how I can get to those hens," he thought, quietly slipping away.

Just before dusk, Cat came back to the farm. This time he was dressed in a long white coat, like a vet, buttoned right up to his neck. He wore a pair of glasses, perched on the tip of his nose, and his ears were hidden beneath a hat. Cat strode up to the gate in the fence, walking tall on his two back legs.

"Hello," he said, his voice a gentle purr. "I'm the vet. I hear that two of you are sick. Would you be so kind as to let me in?"

"Of course," said a fat brown hen, and she strutted over, beak up, ready to undo the inside latch.

But the other hens held her back.

"The vet has a tail," they said.

"It's twitching under his coat!"

"Look at his teeth — so sharp and pointed."

"And listen to his voice, the way it purrs."

The hens all thought for a moment. "It's the cat, isn't it? He's come back."

"And what do we know about cats?" asked the oldest hen.

"I've seen the farm cat chasing mice," said one, looking nervous.

"And I've seen him catching birds," added another, nodding her head.

"I've even seen him eat a frog," chimed a third.

"Yuck!" clucked all three. "So slimy."

"Cats are not to be trusted," chorused the hens.

"Nonsense," purred Cat. "I'm a very kind creature. Now open the gate. I'll make you all feel so much better."

"I think we'll be fine," said the oldest hen, "so long as we don't let you in!"

The cat flicked off his hat, shook off his glasses and slipped out from under his coat. "It will have to be mice again, I suppose..." he said.

Moral:
Uninvited visitors are often most welcome when they've gone.

The Lion and the Fox

Lion sighed. His back ached, his paws hurt, even his tail felt sore. "The trouble is," he realized, "I'm getting old." He lay down outside his lair and watched as an antelope leaped past him, nearly brushing his nose with her tail.

"I would have had her for breakfast once," thought Lion. "Now I can't even find the energy to lift my head."

As Lion lay in the morning sun, he realized something would have to be done. "If this is what it's like to be old, I'll never get to eat again. I must come up with a plan..."

"Are you all right, Lion?" asked a passing bird, watching him as he lay with his head on his paws.

Lion shook his head. The bird hopped a little closer. Lion looked up. The bird was now very near his jaws. "I could catch her with my tongue," mused Lion. "I've never seen an animal come this close to me before." Then, in a flash, a plan came to him.

"I'm not feeling very well," moaned Lion. "Not well at all. I'm going to drag myself off to that cave on the hillside and lie there, feeling awful. Of course, it'll be very lonely, being in that cold cave, all alone..."

"Poor Lion," tweeted the bird, her bright eyes full of sympathy.

"Yes," said Lion. "Please tell the other animals, as I would love some company."

With those words he dragged himself off to the cave, covering his smile with his paw.

Lion waited and waited. At last, around midday, a warthog came to see him.

"I've heard you are unwell," said the warthog.

"Oh I am," Lion replied.

Warthog came a little closer.

"Very unwell..." Lion went on.

Warthog came closer still.

"You'll notice my eyes are dull and my mane is lank," said Lion.

As Warthog looked on, Lion seized the moment and pounced. Warthog was so close, he didn't stand a chance.

"Dee~licious," said Lion, smacking his lips. "Oh the joy of a full stomach. My plan is working perfectly."

All that day, animals came to visit Lion — first a hare, then a buffalo, followed by a zebra and a wildebeest. Lion ate them all.

"Trickery gets you everywhere," he thought

to himself. "All these animals are walking straight into my trap. I'm starting to enjoy my old age."

As the days passed, Fox began to notice something strange was happening. Lion was unwell, everyone said. Lots of animals were going to visit him... but none seemed to be coming back.

"I think I'd better find out what's going on," Fox decided. So he set off up the hill to Lion's cave.

"Come in, come in," croaked Lion, from within the dark depths of the cave. "How kind of you to come. Have you heard that I'm unwell? I do so enjoy my visitors."

Fox stepped forward, then looked down at the ground. He looked again and felt the hairs of his coat stand up in shock.

"What are you waiting for, Fox?" asked Lion, testily. "Come in!"

"It's just that I can see lots of footprints going into your cave," remarked Fox, "but none coming out."

"Well isn't that a funny thing," said Lion.

"Funny for you," said Fox. "Not so funny for your visitors. I'd better go and warn the other animals," he added, already backing out.

"Come back!" called Lion. "What are you talking about?"

"Don't pretend you don't know," retorted

Fox. "This lair is a trap. All those who come in have walked straight into your mouth."

"Grrrr," said Lion, then shut his jaws with an angry snap.

Moral:
If you are wise, you will look out for signs of danger.

The Cat and the Mice

The cat sat on the street and watched the house. "Perfect," he purred. "It's just as I heard. The place is infested with mice."

He could see them scurrying in and out, their plump little bodies just asking to be eaten. "I shall have a lovely time here," he thought.

He padded inside the house, licking his lips in delight. There were even more mice than he had imagined — mice in the hallways, mice on the stairs, mice on the mantelpiece, mice sitting on chairs.

The cat walked between them and, *Oh, joy!* They didn't seem to care. "They've never seen a cat before," he realized. "This is going to be a *very* easy lunch."

And he set to work. The cat pounced here, there and everywhere, plucking up the mice in his paws and stuffing as many as he could between his jaws.

When he was full to the brim, he sauntered out again with a grin. "I'll come back in the

morning," he decided. "What fun!"

But when the cat returned, the mice were nowhere to be seen. He was met with empty halls and passageways — not a squeak or a scuttle to be heard. "Mice, mice, come out and play!" he purred. "I'll be nice this time..."

He bent down to peer through the

mouse hole, and was sure he could see hundreds of gleaming eyes, shining in the dark like stars.

"I'll wait," thought the cat. "They'll come out soon enough."

But they didn't... The cat sat there, his tail twitching. "If I pretend to be dead," he mused, "the mice will creep out of their hole and run around me as they did before."

In a flash of fur, he leaped onto a cupboard, let out a startled cry, then stretched himself out – as stiff and still as one dead.

He waited some more, one eye slightly open, to catch a glimpse of the mice.

Inside their hole, the mice waited, breathing fast. "Has he gone?" whispered a little mouse.

"Can we go out again now?"

"It seems quiet out there," added another.

"Would he give up that easily?" asked a third. "You – little mouse – go and see."

With trembling paws, the little mouse crept forward and poked out his head. His eyes darted left and right and he could see nothing. With a sigh of relief he was about to scuttle out when his eye was caught by something large and furry lying on top of a tall cupboard.

"The cat!" he cried.

"Where?" asked the other mice.

"There!" squeaked the little mouse, pointing to the cupboard.

"What's it doing?" asked the others.

"It's just... lying there," said the little mouse, quivering like jelly. "Actually," he went on, "I think it might be dead."

"Dead! Dead!" The mice began leaping around for joy, jostling and squeaking as they headed out of the hole to look.

"Stop!" cried an old mouse. "Don't you know it's a trick, you fools?"

The mice stopped in their tracks. "A trick?" they asked.

"Yes," sighed the old mouse. "Stand back and I'll show you."

The others cleared the way. The old mouse hobbled over to the hole, stood on his two back legs and looked directly at the cat. "You can lie there as long as you like, pretending to be dead," he said. "But we're not coming out. We know your wicked ways."

The cat stirred. "So I see," he said. "Oh well. I suppose, then, I'll be on my way."

Open~mouthed, the mice watched him go.

"But... but..." gasped the little mouse. "How did you know?"

"A simple rule," said the wise old mouse. "Never trust the wicked."

Moral:
Once bitten, twice shy.

The Wolf and the Heron

Wolf was a dangerous animal, no doubt about it: sharp teeth, sharp claws, sharp eyes. No one wanted to go near Wolf, not if they could help it. As for Wolf – he prowled and he pounced and he scavenged his meals. He wasn't around to make friends. Not, that is, until he got a bone stuck in his throat.

That bone itched and it scratched and it tickled, and no matter how much he coughed, it wouldn't come up. "Argh!" rasped Wolf. "I can't live like this. I don't want to eat, I don't want to hunt. I just need to get rid of this cursed bone!"

Wolf looked everywhere for help. He asked the deer and the ants and the snakes, even the birds in the trees. They all shook their heads. "We're not going near you," they said.

At last, Wolf met a heron, who agreed to remove the bone for a fee. "Five gold coins should cover it," said Heron.

Wolf opened his jaws wide and Heron stuck his neck right in. He reached all the way down

Wolf's throat and plucked
out the bone with his beak.

"My money, please,"
said Heron.

Wolf gave a snarly
laugh. "No money for
you, old bird. Isn't it enough
that you put your head in a
wolf's throat... and lived!"

"What trick is this?" cried Heron.

"Not a trick," said Wolf, "but a lesson."

Moral:
Don't expect rewards from the wicked.

GREED

The Goose that Laid the Golden Eggs

Deep in the woods stood a little cottage. It was so tumbledown, it looked as if it were growing back into the ground. Ivy encrusted the walls, flowers sprouted out of the roof and mice ran in and out of the door. Inside, on a straw~covered floor, sat a snow~white goose, cackling away as she laid an egg.

A man rushed into the room. "At last," he cried. "We can have our supper."

His wife brought out the frying pan and placed it over the fire, while the man slid his hand under the goose's soft, fluffy down. His fingers closed over something cold and hard. A stone? He sighed as he pulled it out. The object was shaped like an egg, only heavier, harder...

"What is it?" asked his wife.

"I don't know," the man replied. He carried it over to where a ray of sunlight came streaming in through a hole in the roof. The object glittered. They gasped.

"It couldn't be..?" said his wife.

"It is, it really is!" cried the man.

"GOLD!" they shouted gleefully together.
"A golden egg!"

"But how?" asked the man. He looked from
the shiny, sparkling egg to their little white
goose in wonder.

"Never mind how," muttered his wife.
"You must go straight to
market in the morning
and sell it. We're going
to be rich... rich!"

And they began
to dance around their
room, singing and laughing
for joy.

At first light, the man set out through the woods, the egg in his pocket, humming a giddy tune. He wandered through the hustle and bustle of the market, until he found what he wanted – a rickety stall with a large set of scales.

An old man sat behind the counter calling, "Get money for your gold. I'll give you the best price! I'll take necklaces, bracelets, goblets..."

"How much money would I get for this?" asked the man, gingerly taking the golden egg out of his pocket and placing it on the scales.

The old man raised his eyebrows. He picked up his magnifying glass. "Remarkable," he said, studying it closely. "Pure gold. And it's been made to look exactly like an egg! I've never seen anything like it."

He pulled out bag after bag of coins and handed them to the man.

As if in a dream, the man floated from stall to stall, buying everything he wanted and lots of things he didn't, just because he could. He bought dresses for his wife and a fine suit for himself, jewels and flowers, furniture and food. He bought so much there was no way he could carry it all. He spent the last of his money on a donkey and cart, loaded up his goods and rode home in triumph.

His wife was delighted. She tried on dress after dress, twirling around as she admired herself in their new gilt mirror. Then they sat

down together and gorged themselves on the delicious food – quails' eggs and caviar, fine wines and exotic fruit.

But as the meal drew to a close, the woman sighed with disappointment.

"I want more," she said hungrily.

"More food?" asked the man in amazement, thinking of all they'd eaten.

"No... more money," said his wife, her eyes glinting. "I want enough money to live in a fine house and to eat like this forever. I want to sleep on silken sheets, eat from golden plates and have jewels dripping from my fingers."

They both looked at their goose hopefully. She began to cackle. They froze, hardly daring to breathe.

"Did she..? Could she have..?" the
woman wondered.

With trembling hands the man reached
under the goose, and his heart sang as once
more he felt the cold, hard shape of a
golden egg.

After that, the goose laid a new golden egg
each day. The man and his wife grew rich and
fat. They left their little cottage and bought a
grand house and as many grand things as they
could to go in it. They had servants by the
dozen, thick velvet carpets, fountains in the
garden and walkways studded with jewels.
But the more they had, the more they wanted...

"I need a team of twenty white horses, pulling a silk~lined carriage," said the woman "And I'm bored with all my dresses. I want to buy some more this minute."

"But our goose only lays one egg a day," the man pointed out. "And the money trickles away like water. We spend it as soon as we get it. You'll just have to wait for the goose to lay more eggs."

His wife went outside to the shed where they now kept their goose. A heavy lock hung from the door, but inside, the goose had been given every luxury — satin cushions to sit on, fresh straw every day and curtains on the windows.

The woman took a good look at the goose, smiling at her and patting her on the head – but all the time she was thinking… "I'm sure that goose is full of gold. It must be sitting in her belly, great big gobbets of it. If we cut her open, we'd get all the gold at once…"

That night she told her husband her plan. "Let's go now, while she's asleep. We'll cut her open and grab all the gold. She won't feel a thing. We'll never have to wait for her to lay another egg."

"What a brilliant idea," agreed the man, and they crept out into the night.

They unlocked the goose's door and quickly cut her open. The woman let out an

angry scream. There was no gold inside the
goose, just meat and bone like any other bird.

"What will we do now?" she asked in
horror, looking at the sorry remains of their
little white goose.

But there was nothing they could do.
With no goose, they had no more golden
eggs, and with no golden eggs, they had no
more money to buy things.

First their servants had to go, then all
their fine things – jewels, furniture, even the
paintings on the walls. Then the house itself
had to be sold, and the man and his wife had
nowhere to go but their tumbledown cottage
in the woods.

The woman kept her dresses, but they grew shabby and ragged. Soon, all they had to remind them of their riches was the empty space on their cottage floor, where their little white goose had once sat and laid her magical golden eggs.

Moral:
Be happy with what you have.

The Fox in the Tree

Fox padded through the snow, feeling very pleased with himself. At dawn he had raided a henhouse and made off with ten hens.

"A personal best," he boasted. "All that's left is a pile of feathers."

And then, just a moment ago, he had waylaid a lovely plump rabbit with a snap of his strong white teeth. "I really have done well," thought

Fox, wearing a satisfied smirk. His stomach felt warm and happy and full.

"I'll go back to my den," he decided, "and have a little nap. After all, I deserve one after such a busy morning."

He hadn't gone far when he caught the most delicious scent on the air. His nostrils twitched. "Mmm... do I smell *more* food?"

He looked around but could see nothing but snow and trees.

"How strange," thought Fox, following the smell to an old oak tree. "It's coming from right inside this tree."

He gently touched the trunk with his paw, then jumped back as the snow fell away,

revealing a
small hole in the
hollow tree. Tucked away inside,
he saw a loaf of bread, a hunk of
cheese and, even more tempting, a
large chunk of meat.

"Oh ho ho!" cried Fox. "It must have
been left here by a shepherd. My luck
is in again." He reached for the food
with his paw, then groaned. It was
just out of reach. He tried again,
straining with every sinew in his
body, but it was no use.

Fox stood back and
thought. "If I can

slink into a henhouse and outrun a rabbit,
I must be able to get my paws on this meal.
Nothing's going to outfox this fox."

He looked at the hole in the tree, then
looked again. "It's not too high, or too small,"
he told himself. "I *could* squeeze through it."

He poked his head through the hole, then
followed with his body, which rubbed against
the side of the tree. But, with a wiggle and a
squirm, he was in.

"Hooray!" cried Fox. Without waiting a
moment longer, he wolfed down the food in
greedy gulps.

"Aah!" he said, licking his lips. "Very
satisfactory. Time to go."

He poked out his head and his front legs and pulled... but his body stayed just where it was.

"If I could get in, I must be able to get out," reasoned Fox, and he heaved and squeezed some more. Nothing happened. His bloated stomach wouldn't budge.

He twisted this way and that, his body writhing like an eel, but no matter which way he moved he couldn't get out.

"Help!" he cried. "Help! I'm... stuck."

Soon, a whisper was spreading through the woods, from rabbits to squirrels to birds to moles. "Fox is stuck in a hole. *Ha ha ha. Hee hee hee.* Quick, quick. Come and see."

The woodland animals crept out from their homes and gathered around the hollow oak tree, all staring up at Fox.

"You're stuck?" they giggled.

"Not so scary now, is he?" whispered the baby rabbits.

"What happened?" asked a brave mole.

Fox glared at them all. "I came in here to get some food," he snapped. "And now I can't get out again."

"He got what he deserved," squeaked a fieldmouse. Everyone laughed.

Fox ground his teeth but managed not to lose his temper. "If you could just pull my paws," he said stiffly, "then I think you might be able to free me."

None of the animals moved.

"You two, over there!" said Fox, pointing to a couple of rabbits. "Come and help me."

The rabbits shook their heads. "Why should we help you?" they asked. "All you do is eat us."

"I'm not going to eat you *now*," said Fox impatiently.

Still, no one moved.

"Is no one going to pull me out of here?"

The animals shook their heads.

"Then what am I going to do?" Fox wailed.

A rabbit bounded up to him. "You'll just have to wait until you're thin enough to come

out again."

"That's what comes of being so greedy," added a squirrel, gleefully.

Fox waited and waited, eating nothing, only allowing rainwater to pass his lips. Then, on the third day, a very grumpy and rather thinner Fox, squeezed his way out of the hole at last.

Moral:
Don't be greedy.

The Dog and the Bone

"Stop! Thief!" cried the butcher, and he dived after the dog. But he was too late. The dog bounded out of his shop, a juicy bone gripped in his great big jaws.

The butcher set off after him. "Come back, you scoundrel!" he yelled.

The dog bounded on, past the bakery and down the street.

"Help me!" called the butcher. And the baker came running out of his shop and joined in the chase. The dog was an old enemy, always stealing his freshly~baked cakes.

"Stop! Thief!" they cried together.

But even with the two of them chasing, they couldn't catch the dog, who ran on, around the corner and past the grocer's shop, his paws pounding over the ground.

"Help us!" called the butcher and the baker.

Out came the grocer to join in

the chase.

Now the dog was wagging his tail, full of glee. "They'll never catch me," he thought. "I'm the fastest hound in town."

And he ran on, his sights set on the safety of the woods beyond.

"He's getting away," panted the grocer. "We'll lose him in all those trees."

At the end of the field the butcher leaped, his outstretched fingers reaching for that teasing tail. He missed.

The baker crashed into the back of the butcher, the grocer banged into them both, and they all toppled over in a tangled heap.

"Stop... Thief!" they cried one last time, as the dog glanced over his shoulder, grinned... and was gone, away into the woods with his juicy bone.

"I'll take it to a snug little cave," thought the dog, "where I can munch it and crunch it all I want, undisturbed. Oh... it'll be so delicious." On that happy thought, he began to drool.

"Hello dog," said a passing fox. Seeing the large bone in the dog's mouth, he stopped. "Look how much meat's on that bone!" he said. "I'm so hungry. Could you give me just a little piece?"

The dog growled, shook his head and walked on.

"Oooh," said a wolf, as the dog padded past his lair. "Please, please share. I have so many cubs to feed…"

The dog growled, shook his head and walked on.

"This meat is mine," he thought greedily. "All mine!"

He stopped only when he reached a wide river, looking for a place to cross. "It's my lucky day," the dog decided, for there, just to his left, was a little arched bridge.

"Perfect!" laughed the dog.

Slowly and carefully, he began to cross. He placed one paw in front of the other, all the time gripping the bone in his mouth. But the bridge began to wobble.

In fear, the dog looked down into the water, and there... he couldn't believe it! Another dog was staring back at him, with an even bigger bone in its mouth. He growled, drew back his lips and bared his teeth.

The dog in the water did the same.

"I want that bone," thought the dog. "How dare he have a bigger bone than me!"

He swiped at the dog in the water.

The dog in the water swiped back.

The dog could bear it no longer. "Give that bone to me!" he growled. With a fierce bark, he opened his mouth wide... his great juicy bone fell from his jaws and dropped into the river.

But the dog didn't go after it. Instead, he leaped at the dog in the water.

He dived this way and that, searching for
the other dog. Where had it
gone? He swam around
and around, dived
down, bobbed back up...
where was that other dog hiding?

Soon he began to tire, his breath coming
in great pants as he fought against the river's
current. At last, he had to haul himself over to
the muddy bank to rest.

"I've lost my bone," he moaned. "It's all
that other dog's fault. Teasing me like that,
grinning at me with his great chunk of meat..."

He peered into the river again, to see if he
could find him.

Another dog stared back, its mouth empty, its eyes angry. That was when he realized. He had leaped at his own reflection. He had tried to steal his own bone. He had tricked himself out of his supper.

"I'm a greedy fool," he groaned.

Moral:
Be satisfied with what you have.

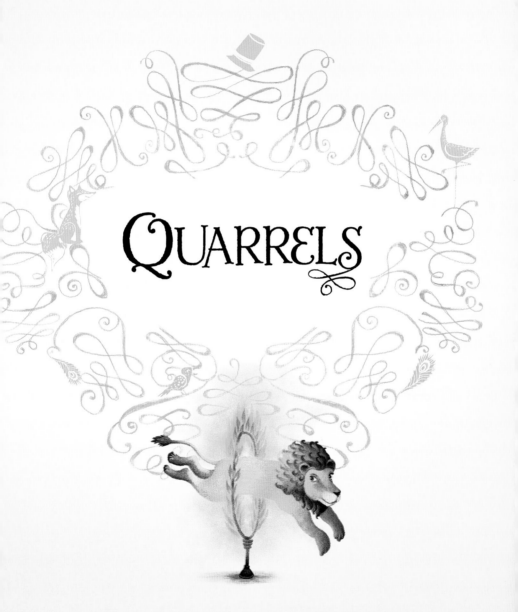

QUARRELS

The Sun and the Wind

The North Wind was showing off.
He blew over the sea, whipping it up
into a frenzy of spitting spray and rolling,
rollicking waves. He tossed ships in the air
as if it were child's play.

"Look at me!" he cried. "So wild and free.
I am the strongest of them all."

From high in the sky, the Sun watched
him and laughed to herself. "That Wind..."
she thought, "that bragging, big~headed,
arrogant Wind. Does he really think he's
stronger than me? He doesn't know the
meaning of strength."

"You're nothing but a tiresome boy,"
she called out. "I am the Sun and I'm
stronger by far."

"Oh really?" taunted the Wind. "Watch
this!" And he tore over the land, snapping off
branches and pinging back trees like elastic
bands. He plucked roofs from houses, blasted

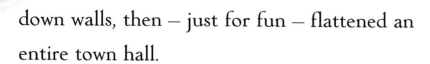

down walls, then — just for fun — flattened an entire town hall.

The Sun sneered. "Is that the best you can do?" she asked.

"Ha!" said the Wind. "I haven't even started. In fact, I think we should have a contest! You'll soon see how much stronger I am. After all, you do nothing but sit in the sky all day."

"A contest?" said the Sun. "What a good idea. Let me see…" and she gazed down on the world below, until her eye was caught by a man, walking along with a bag on his back, on a path near the sea.

"The first to strip that man of his clothes is

the winner," declared the Sun. "Do you think you can do it?"

"Easily," retorted the Wind. "Watch and learn, lazy Sun. I'll show you just how it's done."

The Wind wafted down to the man and pulled at his scarf. At first he tugged it — a gentle tease — then with a whoosh he sent it sailing away in the breeze.

"Come back!" shouted the man. He leaped, but too late, as the Wind entangled the scarf in a tree.

The Wind chuckled. "And for my next trick..." He whisked the hat from the man's head and blew it effortlessly out to sea.

"I told you it would be easy," jeered the Wind.

The Sun looked unconcerned. "You're not done yet," she said.

Next, the Wind bore down on the man with a blast of his freezing breath. The man was buffeted this way and that, his coat flapping wildly, as if it had grown great blue wings. It was nearly ripped right from him, but with flailing hands the man grappled with it and hung on tight. The Wind puffed out his cheeks and blew harder still, but the harder he blew, the more the man clung on.

The Wind paused, forced to catch his breath. The man seized his chance and opened

his bag, pulling on yet more clothes — a pair of gloves and another coat, which he buttoned up to his neck.

The Sun smiled. "You've had your chance," she said. "My turn now."

"Humph," said the Wind, reluctantly drawing back.

The Sun shone down, radiating gentle warmth. The man quickly took off his gloves and extra coat. The Sun smirked. Then she darted burning rays down to the ground, until the air sizzled with heat. The man grew red. Beads of sweat appeared on his brow and he gazed longingly at the sparkling sea. In a moment, he threw off his clothes and ran, naked, into the welcoming waves.

"You see!" said the Sun, gloatingly. "I won easily. For all your huffing and puffing, you were powerless. All he needed was some gentle persuasion."

The Wind snorted with rage. "You may have won but I can still have fun."

And while the man swam in the sea, the Wind flew off with his clothes.

Moral:
Persuasion is better than force.

The Lion and the Statue

"This way, this way!" called the man in the top hat. "Ziggi's Circus has come to town! Come see our lion jump through rings of fire! Admire our dancing dogs, our prancing horses, our juggling monkeys... Be amazed by our acrobats... Laugh at our clowns... Ziggi's Circus has come to town!"

The crowd surged past the circus man, talking excitedly, promising to come to the show that evening. They gazed with pleasure at the big top, a vast tent with rainbow flags fluttering in the summer breeze.

Behind the tent, in a metal cage, sat the circus lion. "Another town... another act," he moaned. "I hate the circus. How I long for Africa, for days spent basking in the sun..."

"But you're our star performer," said the lion tamer, his voice soft like butter, comforting, cajoling. "What would we do without you? Everyone adores it when you jump through hoops and balance on balls."

"And what about me?" said the lion, miserably.

"Do you think I love it? To think I was once king of the jungle. When I stalked the land everyone quaked with fear."

His eyes grew misty at the memory and took on a glint of forgotten pride. Then, for the first time in a long while, he looked the lion tamer in the eye, pulled himself up to his full height and shook out his great mane.

"I'm not going to perform *any more*," he declared.

"Oh yes you are," said the lion tamer, cracking his whip at the sound of such defiance. He leaned close to the cage. "You'll perform tonight, I'll make sure of it. It's always been this way. People are stronger than lions. I can make you do whatever I want."

"People are stronger than lions?" scoffed the lion. "What a ridiculous thing to say. If I wasn't chained up, I could crush you like a strawberry with my paw."

The lion tamer laughed. "Then why do you think I'm standing free and you're trapped in this cage? Of course I'm stronger than you."

The lion stared at the man, scornfully.

"I'll prove it to you," said the lion tamer. He opened the lion's cage and cracked his whip. "Now follow me!" he ordered, yanking on the lion's chain.

"This should be interesting," muttered the lion, padding out on his velvet paws.

Together, they walked out of the town, down a winding dirt track that led deep into the countryside.

"Where are we going?" asked the lion, as he was pulled along by his chain.

"Back to the village where I was born," replied the lion tamer.

At last they came to the village, where narrow streets led to a paved square. There, in the middle of the square, stood a stone statue, raised up for all to see.

"Look!" said the lion tamer, pointing proudly at the statue. "Proof! People *are* stronger than lions."

The lion looked at the statue.

It showed a man and a lion fighting, with the man on top, sword held high, ready to plunge it into the terrified lion.

The lion merely smiled. "You think the statue tells the truth?" he asked. "What if lions could make statues? Then, I think, you'd see plenty of men under our paws."

The lion tamer looked shocked, as if he'd never thought of that before. Then he looked at the lion, teeth bared, red tongue showing. He backed away, cracking his whip again and again to mask his trembling hands.

"Stay there, I tell you," he shouted at the lion. "Don't come any closer." For the first time he took in the lion's great size. He looked

so much bigger now he was out of his cage.
The lion's teeth gleamed white in the
sunshine. "They're as sharp as knives,"
thought the lion tamer. Then he looked
down at the lion's velvet paws and gulped
as he saw his dagger~like claws.

The lion smiled
again, then raised his
huge paw high in the
air, right above the
lion tamer's head,
claws at the ready.
He roared.

The lion tamer
turned and fled.

The lion looked once more at the old stone statue and smiled. "It's funny," he thought, "how much men like to believe their own lies." Then he shook his head and padded out of the square, down the twisting streets, and out into the open air of the countryside — free at last.

Moral:

The story depends on the teller.

The Fox and the Stork

Fox was a trickster. He played tricks on everybody — Bear and Crow, Wolf and Raven.

"You must stop," said his friend, Stork. "Not everyone enjoys your tricks."

"Yes they do," said Fox. "Everyone loves them. They think I'm funny."

"Do you think you'd find it funny if we played a trick on you?" asked Stork.

"Of course I would," retorted Fox.

Not long after, Fox decided it was high time he played a trick on Stork. "Would you like to come for supper?" he asked. "I'll make you a feast fit for a king."

"Thank you," Stork replied. She hadn't noticed the glint in Fox's eyes.

Stork spent all day dreaming about the delicious food Fox might give her. "Perhaps it will be frogs in pondweed sauce? Or fresh fish sprinkled with herbs?"

She decided only to have a very light lunch of dragonflies, so as to leave lots of room for her supper.

Stork arrived promptly at Fox's den at six o'clock, with neatly brushed feathers and a clean beak.

"Welcome! Welcome!" said Fox. "Sit down, my dear. I do hope you like it."

Stork sat down on her chair and patted her stomach with her wing. "How exciting," she said. "I'm famished."

With a flourish, Fox brought over two shallow bowls and filled them with a mouth~watering fish soup.

"Help yourself," said Fox, beginning to lap up the soup with his tongue.

Stork looked at the bowl. It was too shallow,

she realized, and her beak was too long. She put her head this way and that, but no matter what she did, she couldn't drink any of the soup – only wet the end of her beak.

Stork looked up and saw Fox's eyes sparkle with mischief. "I'm so sorry," he said, getting up. "Is the soup not to your liking? Let me take it away."

"Not at all," said Stork smoothly, rising from her chair. "It was so kind of you to invite me. I would love you to come to mine for supper. Shall we say next week?"

A time was agreed and Stork left the den, secretly, silently fuming. "I'll show that Fox," she vowed.

A week later, Fox tapped on Stork's door in time for supper.

"Welcome, dear friend," said Stork, smiling at him. "Come in and sit down."

Fox was chuckling to himself, remembering how well he had tricked Stork. He sat down at the table and looked at the tall jar in front of him. "It smells delicious," he remarked.

"I hope you're hungry," said Stork. "I've made some soup too, just like you. It's fresh watercress."

She put her beak in the jar and began to slurp up the soup.

Fox put his snout in the jar, but quickly realized it was far too short to reach the soup.

He tried to lift the jar up, but it was too heavy for him to hold. All he could do was lick a few drops from the rim.

Stork finished her soup. "Oh, I'm so sorry," she said. "Didn't you like it?"

"It's not fair," fumed Fox. "What a terrible trick to play. I'm starving."

"Well now you've learned your lesson," said Stork. "Don't play tricks on your friends."

Moral:

Do as you would be done by.

The Lion and the Wild Boar

The sun beat down, hotter and hotter and hotter. Some animals sat panting in the shade, while others drank from a shrinking waterhole. Wild Boar, meanwhile, trotted off to a secret spring he had discovered, tucked away in a hidden corner of the plains. He stumbled over dusty ground, tongue lolling, eager with thirst.

"I'd much rather drink here than at the waterhole," he thought. "It's so much nicer to have the spring to myself."

But when he got there, he found Lion, already drinking the water.

"What are you doing here?" demanded Wild Boar. "This is my spring."

"I got here first," snarled Lion, padding towards him.

"Then it's time for you to leave," Wild Boar replied.

Lion roared and bared his teeth.

Wild Boar brandished his tusks.

The next moment, they charged.

Lion swiped at Wild Boar with his lethal claws. Wild Boar leaped out of the way, then turned on Lion, piercing him with his tusks. The two animals circled each other, dodging and snarling, roaring and grunting.

"I'm going to keep fighting until you leave," said Lion.

"And I'm going to do the same," vowed Wild Boar.

As their battle raged on, the animals began to tire. Wild Boar was panting heavily and blood dripped from Lion's side.

They both paused for a moment, forced to

catch their breath. Lion looked up at the sky and saw vultures circling overhead.

Silently, he raised his paw and pointed. Wild Boar looked up too. He knew why the vultures were there. "They're waiting for us to kill each other," he said.

"I know," said Lion, nodding. "They want to eat whichever one of us dies first."

"I don't want to become food for a vulture," said Wild Boar. "Surely it would be better for us to be friends?"

"I agree," said Lion, smiling. He sheathed his claws. Wild Boar lowered his tusks. Together, they stumbled over to the spring and drank long and deep.

High in the sky, the vultures watched them. Then, with a sigh, they flapped their great fringed wings and soared away.

Moral:
Put an end to quarrels or everyone will suffer.

FRIENDSHIP

The Town Mouse and the Country Mouse

The Country Mouse lay in the corn field, staring up at the summer sky. He could see the swifts and swallows high above him, soaring over the treetops. He knew when summer ended they would fly far, far away, to countries he had never heard or dreamed of.

"But that's not for me," he said to himself,
pattering back to his little cottage in the hedge.
He thought fondly of his smooth earthy walls, his
fireplace, his soft, grassy floor.

He reached his hedge and there, arms opened
wide, was his friend, the Town Mouse.

"Surprise!" he cried. "I thought I'd come and
see you. It's been so long."

The Country Mouse beamed from ear to ear.
"Come in, come in," he said, pushing open his
small wooden door.

The Town Mouse sat on a logpile chair while
the Country Mouse bustled about, looking for
food for his friend to eat.

"I've not got much," he muttered. "Just a few

ears of corn, and some husks of barley."

"Is that all?" cried the Town Mouse, looking disappointed.

"Next month I'll have nuts and blackberries," the Country Mouse chattered on.

The Town Mouse shook his head. "You live like an ant, my friend," he said. "Come home with me. We'll eat like kings."

They set off together, scurrying through hedgerows, along river banks, into the hustle and bustle of town.

"This way," said the Town Mouse, beckoning the Country Mouse into his house. They scampered straight to the kitchen, and there... in the cupboard...

"You have beans and cheese and honey and fruit!" cried the Country Mouse, skipping from one to the other, tasting, feasting, nibbling, gnawing. "I'll never go home again," he sighed.

Just then, the door began to open. A large
hand reached into the cupboard. The Country
Mouse screamed.

"Run!" cried the Town Mouse. "Quick! Into
this hole."

The Country Mouse followed, whiskers
quivering. "We were nearly caught!"

"Nonsense," scoffed the Town Mouse.
"Now come with me to the dining room. Just
wait till you see the food there."

A feast met the Country Mouse's eyes and
he soon forgot his fears. He lapped up cream,
trailed his paw in chocolate sauce and sank his
teeth into cookies. He shut his eyes in blissful
contentment, when, creak, creak, creak...

the door swung open and a maid came in.

"Mice! Mice!" she screamed.

Swat! Swat! went her mop.

The Town Mouse grabbed his friend
by the ear and pulled him to safety beneath
a chair.

"We must run from here to the hole in the
wall," he said. "Go as fast as you can, but watch
out for stomping feet."

The Country Mouse ran. He could feel his
heart beating, he could hear his breath coming
in heavy pants. He thought he might burst
with fear.

"You call this place home?" he cried when
he reached the hole. "I know you have every

luxury, but think of the dangers! I'd rather have the peace and quiet of the country any day."

"You're going back?" said the Town Mouse. "To that hole in the hedge?"

The Country Mouse nodded his head. "Farewell, my friend. It's the simple life I want," he said.

Moral:
It is better to live simply in peace than in luxury and fear.

The Ant and the Dove

Ant was thirsty, but the path down to the stream was steep and the stream itself flowed fast and deep. Ant knew he would have to be careful, but he was desperate for a drink.

He crept down the bank, keeping close to the ground, then clambered onto a blade of grass that arched above the water.

"I'll be safe here," he told himself, gripping the grass with his legs. Then along came a sudden gust of wind.

Ant screamed. He tried to hold on but the wind was too strong. He sailed through the air, a little brown dot with flailing legs, until... SPLISH!

The stream carried him this way and that. The burbling water tumbled over him, pushing him down. He bobbed back up again, gasping for breath.

"Help!" cried Ant. "Help!"

He never thought anyone would hear him, his voice a faint whisper drowned out by the

rushing water. But then, looking up, he saw a dove circling overhead, as if she were trying to find a way to help. He watched as she flew over to a nearby tree, snapped off a twig from a branch then swooped down to the water. Gently, she dropped the twig in.

With the last of his strength, Ant swam over to the twig and clung on. He was swept past rocks and down waterfalls, until at last he came to rest by the side of the stream. Ant tottered from the twig and kissed the ground, relieved to be on dry land once more.

"Oh that was close!" he muttered. "The water nearly had me there. If it hadn't been for that dove, for that dear, kind dove..."

He looked around, wishing to thank her, only to see a man standing above him on the bank. He had a net in his hand, and the dove was in it.

"Oh no!" thought Ant. "A bird~catcher!"

The dove was fluttering wildly inside the net, beating her wings as she tried to escape, but the man only laughed and gripped the net tighter.

Ant scurried over as fast as he could. "I must get there in time, I must..." he thought.

When he reached the man, he scampered over his shoe and up his leg. Then he bit him, as hard as he could.

Ant heard the man scream and scuttled out

again. The man had dropped the net and the dove was nowhere to be seen. Quickly, Ant ran on, until he reached an old oak tree. He scurried up its gnarly bark, and there, from an outstretched branch, looked out. In the distance, he could just see the dove, flying free.

"I saved her," thought Ant, with a smile, "just as she saved me."

Moral:
One good turn deserves another.

The
Explorers
and the
Bear

Two friends were walking down a path. They were explorers and had walked over half the world together — through jungles thick with tangled trees, across parched desert lands and up icy mountain peaks. They thought they knew everything there was to know about each other.

It was a calm day. There was no wind and very little sound but for the crackle of twigs underfoot as they walked through a woody glade. Then the stillness was broken by a pounding sound, the noise of four heavy paws coming closer... and closer...

One of the friends turned. "A bear!" he cried. "It's a bear."

He ran to the nearest tree and climbed it, never turning back to look out for his friend, just grabbing the branches in a frenzy and hauling himself up and up, out of danger.

His friend was frozen to the spot. He wanted to run but his legs wouldn't move. He remembered hearing somewhere that a bear wouldn't eat what was already dead. He forced himself to drop to the ground, lying as still as he could, praying that what he had heard was true.

A moment later he felt the bear's hot breath on his neck. He could hear it sniffing him, hear the heavy pants coming from its huge body. The man held his breath. The bear's muzzle moved over his face. Its fur was wet around its mouth, brushing against his ear.

Its pants were loud, so loud they were all he could hear. "It sounds like the sea," he thought.

A moment later, the bear was gone.

The man lay there for a little while, just to

be sure. Then he hauled himself up, feeling dizzy to be still alive.

His friend scrambled down from the tree, leaves and twigs sticking out from his hair at crazy angles. "What did the bear say to you?" he asked.

"What do you mean?" asked the man.

"I saw him whisper in your ear," replied his friend. "He spoke to you – I'm sure of it."

The man allowed himself a slow smile. "That I should avoid men who flee when danger comes," he said.

Moral:
A true friend will face danger at your side.

The Lion and the Mouse

The mouse ran as fast as she could.
The bird was after her — she was sure of it.
Its wide, dark wings hovered above her in the
sky, their shadow blotting out her own on
the ground.

Here and there lay little clumps of withered
grass, and the mouse darted between them,
desperately seeking cover. "It'll swoop at any
moment," she thought to herself. "If only I

could find a place to hide..." Then, ahead, to her relief, she glimpsed a tree, its snaking roots covering the ground like grasping fingers.

"If I can just make it to the tree," thought the mouse. And she ran on, whiskers twitching, paws scurrying, heart pounding. But just as she reached the edge of the tree, the bird folded back its wings, and dived.

The mouse leaped, paws outstretched and landed on a soft, warm mound. She couldn't help it, she had to look – certain the last thing she'd see would be the bird's sharp beak opening wide. Instead she heard a frightened caw, and the bird shot away, its large wings flapping wildly.

"Hooray!" cried the mouse, dancing up
and down. The soft mound seemed to move
beneath her, but the mouse didn't stop to
wonder why. Instead she scurried on, up and up
through what seemed like very strange grass,
short and yellow and then long and tangled
and then, "Oh!" she cried, bouncing down and
landing on something black, wet and cold.
The mouse turned around. She was,
unmistakably, sitting on a lion's nose.

There was a pause. The lion
snored. "He's asleep!" realized
the mouse. "If I can just..."
AAAATCHOOOO!
As the lion sneezed,

his eyes snapped open. He took one look at the startled mouse and roared. "How dare you wake me?" His paw shot out and he snatched up the mouse by her tail.

"I normally wouldn't waste my time eating something as small as you," snarled the lion, "but today I think I'll make an exception." He smacked his lips and the mouse caught a glimpse of a long pink tongue sliding out between terrifying teeth.

"Oh help!" gulped the mouse, feeling sure she was about to be crunched. "Please, please," she begged, putting her paws together and trying to steady her voice as she swayed above the lion's jaws. "Don't eat me. Spare my life

today and one day, I promise to save yours."

The lion laughed. He laughed and laughed, rolling on his back and clutching his stomach as if he were about to burst.

"*You* save *me?*" he scoffed. "That could never happen. Do you have any idea how small and insignificant you are? I could send you flying with a flick of my claw, squish you with the slightest pressure from my paw..."

The mouse waited, willing the end to come quickly, but instead, to her astonishment, the lion set her down on the ground.

"Perhaps," he drawled, "I won't eat you after all. You have made me laugh, little mouse. *You* save *me!*" He chuckled some more.

"Now go," he ordered, "before I change my mind. And don't you dare wake me from my slumbers again!"

The mouse ran. She scampered all the way home to her hole in the ground without stopping once and when she got there, she stayed there, trembling all the way from her tail to her whiskers.

Days passed. The lion hunted at night and slept in the shade of the tree by day, or walked lazily across the grassy plains, shaking his mane so it stood full and proud. He was King of the Beasts and he knew it. He was scared of nothing and no one. Until... SNAP! He walked straight into a hunter's trap.

It was made of heavy
rope and it held him as tight
as ten snakes. No matter
how he struggled, he couldn't get
out. The lion roared in anger and
frustration, tears of rage pouring
down his golden fur. He knew that
when morning came, the hunter
would come and claim him as his prize with
one shot from his gun. Nothing, he thought,
could save him now.

Far away, across that grassy plain, the mouse
came out of her hole, her little ears twitching.
The sound of the lion's roar reached her and all
at once she remembered her promise... *save my*

life today and one day, I'll save yours.

"The lion's in trouble! I must go to him," she told herself. Following the sound of the lion's cries, the mouse ran as if for her own life. She reached him just as dusk was falling, the sky lit like a dying fire by the setting sun. The lion was groaning feebly now, the net close around him like a second skin.

"I've come to help!" said the mouse.

The lion raised his eyes, his expression blank. "What can you do, little mouse? If I can't escape from this trap, no one can help me."

The mouse ignored him and set to work. All night long she nibbled and gnawed at the ropes. She worked fast, scurrying from one spot to the next, never pausing for an instant, even as her body grew weary.

By morning, as the first light filled the sky, the thick ropes of the net had become as thin as the string on a spider's web. The lion stretched and arched his back. One by one, the last pieces of the net snapped.

Stepping forward, the lion shook out his mane and opened his great jaws wide, as if he were about to swallow the sky. "I'm free!" he roared. "I'm free."

As his voice echoed across the plains, creatures everywhere stopped for a moment and stood still. They knew it for the sound of

the king of the beasts. "Listen to how terrible he is!" they whispered to one another.

What have I done? thought the mouse, filled for a moment with fear. *Did I really dare to set the lion free? Surely, he will eat me now.*

Once again, the mouse found herself trembling before him. She looked up, saw his great mane bristling, his whole body packed with power, his eyes black as night.

The lion looked down at the quivering mouse. "Thank you," he said. "I see I was wrong. You came to me when I was in trouble. Little friends can be great friends indeed."

He gently held out his paw. "Climb aboard!" he said with a smile. "Together, we can walk across the plains."

So the mouse scurried up the lion's back and watched the sunrise as never before, while all the other animals looked on in wonder, to see a lion who was friends with a mouse.

Moral:
The strong can depend on the weak.

CUNNING

The Crow and the Jug

Crow flew for miles, his black, fringed wings like long fingers, sifting through the sky. He was searching for water. It hadn't rained for months and from up high he could see dusty riverbeds, winding like worms through the cracked earth.

At last, he came to a garden, where faded grass grew in raggedy patches and trees still clung to the last of their leaves.

"There might be water here," thought Crow.

He swooped down, then hopped about, peering
into flowerpots and watering cans, full of hope.
But they were empty, nothing inside them but
dust and stones and empty snail shells, rattling
together like old bones.

"Curses," he croaked.

Then, out of the corner of his eye, he
spotted an old jug sitting in the shade. Crow
jumped up to the rim, looked in and gave a
cry of delight. His reflection looked cheerfully
back at him. He'd found water at last.

He bent his head to drink. The jug had a
narrow rim and only the top of his head could
fit in...

"CAW! CAW! CAW!" he called in anger.

The water was too far down for his beak to reach. He couldn't drink a drop.

Crow stopped to think.

"I know! I'll push the jug over. That way the water will come pouring out."

He leaned against the jug with all his might, but it wouldn't budge.

"You're too weak, that's your problem."

Crow jumped around to see an enormous rat, watching him.

"There's water in there, isn't there?" rasped the rat, rubbing his paws together.

Crow nodded. "Yes," he croaked. "There is. And I must drink some soon or I'll die of thirst."

"Then I'll help you push the jug over,"

replied the rat. "We can share the spoils."

The rat rose up on his hind legs, placed his paws against the jug and began to push.

"Wait!" cried Crow. "NO!"

The rat stopped. "Why ever not?"

"If the water goes into the ground, it'll drain away," Crow explained. "We'll have to think of another way."

The rat paused and thought for a few seconds. "There isn't one," he replied. Shrugging his shoulders, he scuttled away.

But Crow refused to give up. "If I can't get

to the water," he thought, "the water will just have to come to me."

He hopped over to the path, picked up a pebble and plopped it into the jug.

He did it again... and again...

Splish!

Splash!

Splosh!

Then he peered in.

The pebbles were pushing up the water. He could almost reach it now.

"It's working!"

he cried, flapping his wings. "It's really working."

Pebble followed pebble until the water had risen to the very top.

Crow bent his head and dipped his beak in. "Ah... Bliss!" he thought. The water trickled down his parched throat, sweeter than syrup, more precious than gold. He drank every last life~giving drop.

Moral:
A problem's not a problem if you
take the time to think.

The Fox and the Billy Goat

Fox was daydreaming as he trotted along. He was thinking of all the plump little hens he'd caught last night, waiting for him in his nice warm den. "I'll go home right now and eat them," he decided. "Then I'll have a little snooze and – Aaaaaargh!"

Fox had been so busy daydreaming, he hadn't noticed the large well. He fell...

Down...

Down...

Down...

Until SPLASH!

"Oh no," groaned Fox. "How will I ever get out of here? And it's so cold and so damp and so dark..."

"Hello," called a voice from above. Fox looked up to see a billy goat, his horned head poking over the top of the well.

"Is the water good down there?" asked the billy goat.

Fox thought fast. *If I can get the billy goat into the well, I can climb up him and get out again...*

"Oh yes, very good," Fox replied. "Fresh and clear and clean."

"Really?" asked the billy goat.

"Really," said Fox. "You should come down and try it."

The billy goat began to climb down the well, clinging with his nimble hooves to the cracks in the rocks. But even the goat — an excellent

climber, used to scaling the trickiest slopes —
couldn't manage the last part. He slipped and
slithered on the damp moss that lined the walls
and came tumbling down with a SPLOSH!

The billy goat just laughed, bent his head
and began to drink. It was only when he had
finished that he began to look around.

"Um... Fox," he said at last. "How do you
think we will get out of here?"

"I have a cunning plan," said Fox. "If you
put your front feet up against the wall and hold
your head high, I'll be able to climb onto you
and jump from there. Then, of course, I can
pull you up behind me."

"An excellent idea," said the billy goat.

At once, Fox began to climb, as quickly as he could. He clambered up the billy goat's back and onto his head. From there, he could just reach the top of the well. He pushed off with his back legs and jumped up and out. Then, without a second glance, he was off, scampering away, heading straight for his den.

"Fox!" called the billy goat. "Fox! Fox! Come back here now."

With a sly smile on his face, Fox stopped and turned back again.

"Yes, billy goat?" he called. "Is something

the matter?"

"What about our deal?" demanded the billy goat. "You promised you'd help me get out."

"What a silly billy goat you are," said Fox. "You should never have climbed into the well without first thinking how to get out again."

And with that, Fox trotted back to his den and his hens, and had a very satisfying supper.

Moral:
Think before you act.

Belling the Cat

The clock struck midnight and the moon shone bright. In a grand house on a tree~lined avenue, everyone was fast asleep. Everyone, that is, but the mice. They were hurrying and scurrying up their little stairs inside the walls, whiskers twitching in excitement. Tonight was the night of the Big Meeting.

"I wonder what it can be about?" they said to each other.

"Perhaps we're going to find out who's been stealing the cheese?" said one.

"Or discuss the rats," suggested another.

"Quiet," tutted one of the older mice, as they reached the attic. "The meeting is about to begin."

The attic floor was heaving with mice, all tumbling over each other in a big heap as they took their places. Above them, on a low~slung beam, stood the Chief Mouse.

He listened for a moment to their squeaks and chatter, then raised his paw to silence them.

"We are here tonight to talk about..." He paused for a moment and lowered his voice: "The cat!"

Just at the sound of that word, many of the mice began to tremble, covering their ears with their paws.

"Oh, don't mention him!"

"How he torments us!"

"The way he creeps up on us."

"Only the other day he pounced on my mother's cousin's wife," said a plump mouse, quivering like jelly.

"That's nothing," said her friend. "I heard he took ten mice in the pantry yesterday. Only their tails were left."

"He must be stopped," said the Chief Mouse. "We must find a way."

At once, the mice fell silent, each one thinking as hard as they could.

"We could try talking to him," suggested a motherly~looking mouse. "We could *ask* him to stop eating us?"

"Yes," added another, her eyes shining brightly. "And what if we offer to bring him other food to eat instead? We could steal scraps of meat from the kitchen..."

"The cat doesn't eat us just because he's hungry," pointed out the Chief Mouse. "He catches us because he thinks it's fun."

The mice were quiet for a long time after that. Then, from the back of the attic, a small voice piped up, "I think I've got it! I really do.

I know how we can stop him from catching us."

Everyone turned to see a little mouse jumping up and down, paws waving in the air. "Wait there," he squeaked, "I'll be back in just a minute."

And he was off. The mice waited. They heard the little mouse's feet pattering away, then nothing, then the sound of his feet pattering back again. *Ding-a-ling-ling.* What was that? *Ding-a-ling-ling.* There it was again.

The little mouse reappeared, his paws behind his back. "The cat is so good at catching us because we never hear him," he declared. Then, with a flourish, he brought out a small golden bell on a string.

"If we tie this bell around his neck," the mouse went on, "we'll always be warned. By belling the cat, you see, he'll never be able to catch us again."

All the mice immediately began cheering and clapping, congratulating the little mouse on his brilliant idea. No one saw the Chief Mouse frown.

The little mouse puffed himself out with pride, smiling from ear to ear. The Chief Mouse raised his paw once more, trying to get everyone's attention. The others were too busy celebrating to notice. At last, the Chief Mouse banged his walking stick against the wooden beam of the attic.

"Yes, yes," he said, wearily. "It's a fine idea. But who, I ask, is going to put the bell on the cat?"

The mice looked hopefully at one another. No one so much as uttered a squeak.

"Just as I thought," said the Chief Mouse. "It's one thing to say something should be done, and quite a different matter to do it."

Moral:
Some things are easier said than done.

The Dog on the Roof

The dog slunk out of the house, his eyes drowsy with sleep. It was a balmy evening and the wooden porch made a perfect resting place, its sun~soaked boards still warm from the heat of the day. The dog shook his shaggy coat, yawned, crossed over his paws and flopped down his head. *Bliss*, he thought. *Sleep...*

Then, "Oof!" he cried. A great weight forced the breath from his body. He felt sharp claws digging into his skin, hot breath on his

face. Terrified, the dog opened his eyes to see
an enormous wolf leaning over him. His eyes
were black with hunger, his tongue lagging,
mouth drooling.

"Please!" cried the dog, as the wolf's teeth
came closer, "Don't eat me!"

"Of course I'm going to eat you," snarled
the wolf. "What else do you think I'm going
to do? Cuddle you?"

"I meant... I meant don't eat me yet," said
the dog, thinking fast. "Look how thin I am.
I hardly have any flesh on my bones at all.
What you want is a nice fat animal to eat,
full of juicy red meat."

The wolf looked around, his paws still

pinning the dog to the floor. "I agree, that would be better," he snarled. "But, as you're the only animal here, I think I'll just get on with it and eat you now."

"But I'll be fatter soon," said the dog, quickly. "There's going to be a huge wedding feast. I know I'm going to have plenty of scraps to eat. After that, you won't even recognize me.

I'll be the plumpest dog in town. Wouldn't you much rather eat me then?"

The wolf sat back on his haunches, his eyes glazed over, imagining he was feasting on a fat, juicy hound.

"Yes, I would," he said. "When's the feast?" he added, his voice trembling with greed.

"Next week," said the dog, trying to hide his relief. "Come back then, at supper time, so I can feast all day on the leftovers. I'll be lying here waiting for you, as fat as can be."

"Thank you!" said the wolf and bounded away, already dreaming of his delicious meal.

The week passed slowly for the wolf. He found hardly any food to eat – just the odd bird and a rotten sheep. His stomach rumbled with hunger and he longed for the day he could feast on the fatted dog.

When that day came, the wolf skipped from his lair, as frisky as a spring lamb. He gambolled through the woods, a great grin on his whiskery face.

"Dinner time!" he thought excitedly, as he arrived at the house. The porch was empty, but he waited patiently beside it. "The dog must still be inside. Ooh! I wonder how fat he is now... perhaps so fat I won't need another meal for a month."

At the thought of sitting down to eat a tasty mound of meat, the wolf's mouth began to

water. His stomach rumbled. "And when I've finished eating him, I can crunch his bones. Yum! Yum!"

The wolf waited and waited, but still the dog didn't come. Then, from above, he heard the sound of gentle snoring. Looking up, he spotted the dog at last, sleeping soundly... on the roof.

"Get down here now!" howled the wolf. "I can't reach you up there."

The dog woke at the sound of the wolf's howl. He stretched lazily, showing off his big belly, full of food from the feast. Only then did he look at the wolf, a sly smile on his face.

"You want me to come down, to be eaten?" he said.

The Dog on the Roof

"Yes, yes," snapped the wolf. "Just as we agreed."

The dog laughed. "Why would I do that?" he said. "You've been tricked, Mr. Wolf. You should have eaten me when you had me, not waited for the wedding feast. As for me, I'm never sleeping on that porch again!"

Moral:
Wise people learn from their mistakes.

RETORTS

The Piglet and the Sheep

Small white clouds scudded across the sky. Down in the valleys, sheep munched on tufts of grass, looking like little clouds themselves that had floated down from the blue.

In among the sheep were splashes of pale pink – young pigs, snorting and snuffling and waving their curly tails.

Mostly, the sheep ignored the piglets. The sheep were older, past playing and larking around. They spent their days chomping on the grass, while the piglets tumbled down the hills, rolled in mud and made the young trees wobble as they scratched their backs against the slender trunks.

As the farmer walked among the sheep, they didn't even look up. The piglets were too busy playing to notice him. He moved slowly, leisurely, as if he were just taking a stroll in the hills. He stopped by a group of piglets, grunting in the grass, a smile on his face.

Then, like a snake striking, his arm shot out and he grabbed a piglet by the scruff of its neck, and tucked it under his arm.

The piglet squealed, frantically twisting and turning its little pink body as it tried to escape the man's grasp.

An old ewe looked up. "Stop making such a fuss," she bleated.

The piglet stopped squealing for a moment and stared at her.

"We get caught by the farmer all the time," the ewe went on, "and we never complain. Honestly," she added huffily. "All that noise! Dreadful! The things I have to put up with from you young 'uns..."

"But when the farmer gets hold of me it's for a different reason," retorted the piglet. "With

The Piglet and the Sheep

you he wants your wool and milk. But it's my flesh he's after!"

And with those words the piglet gave a last frantic buck of his back legs. The surprised farmer loosened his hold and the next moment the piglet was off, making his escape up the hill, waving his tail behind him.

Moral:
Sometimes people are right
to make a fuss.

The Lioness and the Vixen

"Come on children, time to come out,"
said the vixen, watching proudly as her cubs
trotted out of the fox hole. She counted
them loudly. "One, two, three, four, five... six!
There you all are."

The cubs followed their mother out into

the dusky dark, walking in a line, heads held high. The vixen kept glancing back to check on them, so much so that...

..."Ooof!" She walked straight into a large and rather glorious lioness.

The fox cubs all fell over each other and lay in a squealing, tangled heap of legs and tails and russet fur.

"Sorry," said the vixen. "I didn't see you standing there."

The lioness said nothing. She stood very still, only the tip of her tail twitching. The vixen decided she didn't like the lioness's haughty stare.

From behind the lioness's legs peered a

little cub, his round ears pricked, his black eyes
curious and full of mischief.

He bounded over to the fox cubs and began
playing with them.

Though younger, he was already larger. He
swatted them lightly with his paws and laughed
as they tumbled to the ground. Then he looked

back at his mother, a grin on his face.

The vixen's fur bristled. "Where are the rest of your cubs?" she asked.

"There is only one," the lioness replied.

"Only one?" scoffed the vixen. "As you can see, I have a fine litter of six."

"Only one," the lioness repeated, "but a lion."

Moral:

Judge by quality not quantity.

The Fox and the Rooster

One moonlit night, a fox crept into a hen coop. He prowled around the hen house, poking his long nose through the windows and scratching at the ground beneath – but there was no way in.

He gave a disappointed sigh and turned to go. He hadn't gone far when he stopped suddenly, ears pricked. What was that noise? Was it a rustle in the branches overhead?

Fox looked up and gave a slow smile, revealing a fine set of sharp teeth.

There in the branches, just out of reach, was a fat and juicy rooster.

"Good news! Good news!" cried Fox.

"Why? What has happened?" asked Rooster.

"King Lion has declared a truce between all animals," said Fox. "Peace on Earth! No beast may hurt any bird. Instead we are all to live in brotherly friendship."

Fox gestured to Rooster with his paw, beckoning him to come down. "Now isn't that nice?" he went on, with an encouraging smile.

"Why don't you come down and celebrate with me?"

"That is very good news," said Rooster, staying firmly in his place. "And," he added, craning his neck, "I see someone coming with whom we can share the good news."

"Who is that?" asked Fox, a little nervously.

"Only my master's dog," replied Rooster. "A great big hound, famous for hunting foxes. But all that is over now, of course."

Rooster began waving his wings. "Over here!" he called. "Come and join us!"

Fox began to slink away.

"What, going so soon?" asked Rooster.

"Don't you want to celebrate the good news with us?"

"I would love to," said Fox. "But the dog may not have heard King Lion's new truce."

And with those words, Fox dashed away into the night.

Moral:
Liars get tangled in
their own lies.

The
Fir Tree
and the
Bramble

A fir tree stood on
the edge of a forest. It was
a beautiful fir — tall and
strong with long green
branches that brushed
the ground in the
breeze. At the bottom
of the fir crouched a
bramble bush. It was

messy and straggly, spiky and ugly.

"And no use at all," pointed out the fir. "All you do is scratch people. No wonder you're despised."

The bramble didn't say a word. It just glowered at the fir.

"As for me..." the fir tree went on, "people love me. At Christmas I'll be taken into someone's home. I'm so beautiful I'll be given lights and tinsel, angels and stars. I'll be worshipped with presents and songs."

The fir tree sighed and waved its branches around. "You must wish you were more like me," it told the bramble. "But sadly for you, that will never be."

The bramble could stand it no more. "You poor thing," it told the fir. "Just wait until the men come with their axes to chop you down, while I'm left standing, wild and free. Then you'll be wishing you'd been born a bramble."

Moral:

It's not always a good thing to be popular.

The Crab and its Mother

The crab watched her son and sighed. He was scuttling up the beach. But was he going forwards like the turtles and the sea gulls and the wading birds? Oh no! The Silly Chump. He was going sideways!

"What are you doing?" she called to him. "That's not how one should move. Why are you walking so one~sided?"

She hurried over to him, waving her claws in the air in despair. When she reached his side she tutted and tapped him lightly with her legs. "Don't you listen to a word I say? I'm always telling you how to walk. But do you listen? Never! Never!"

The other animals began to laugh. The turtles chuckled. The sea gulls cackled. The wading birds snorted and trilled.

"What?" cried the mother crab, turning on

COMEUPPANCE

The Tortoise and the Eagle

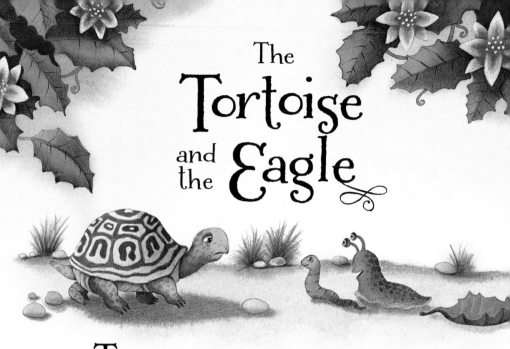

Tortoise wasn't sure he liked being a
tortoise. "I just plod, plod, plod all day," he
moaned.

"At least you have legs," retorted Worm. "I
just slither around on my stomach."

"At least you have a shell," said Slug, "to keep
you dry."

"But I don't care about all that," said Tortoise.

"I want to fly!"

Tortoise began leaping from waterfalls and flapping his legs, but he fell into the river and sank like a stone.

"Tortoises aren't meant to fly," scolded his mother. "Leave it to the birds."

That gave Tortoise an idea. He collected feathers he'd found on the ground and stuck them on his back. Then he went to the highest hill he could find and jumped...

...WEEEEE...

...CRASH!

"You see!" said his mother. "It's just not going to work. You are *not* a bird."

That gave Tortoise another idea. He begged the birds to carry him up to the sky.

"You're too big," chirped the sparrows.

"Too heavy," said the ravens.

"I'll ask Eagle," thought Tortoise. "He'll be

strong enough to carry me."

"No," said Eagle. "Tortoises aren't meant to fly. Everyone knows that. Where are your wings? Where are your feathers? If you fell, you'd shatter your shell."

Tortoise begged and pleaded. He followed Eagle around from dawn till dusk, for days on end until, at last, the mighty bird gave in.

"Just once," said Eagle. He picked Tortoise up by his shell, grasping him in his great claws. Then Eagle flapped his wings and they soared, up, up, up into the airy blue.

Tortoise looked down and gulped. He saw the ground, rushing away from him, with nothing beneath him but air. Everything got smaller and

smaller. He began to tremble and shake.

"What's the matter?" asked Eagle.

"I d~d~don't like it," stammered Tortoise. "I'm scared. Please, Eagle, take me home."

Eagle laughed. "I thought you wanted to fly, little Tortoise?"

"I did," said Tortoise. "But now I don't. It's t~t~terrifying."

Eagle flapped his wings and turned a graceful arc in the air. Then he sliced through the sky like a scythe, head bent, wings folded, sailing down, down, down to the ground. He dropped Tortoise just by his mother.

Tortoise tottered from his grasp, then lay flat on the grass, hugging it to him. "Oh the ground! The ground!" he sang. "I love being close to it. I love going slowly. I'm so glad I'm a tortoise."

"You wouldn't rather be an eagle?" said his mother, amazed.

"No," Tortoise replied. "I'm happy – just as I am."

Moral:
Be careful what you wish for.

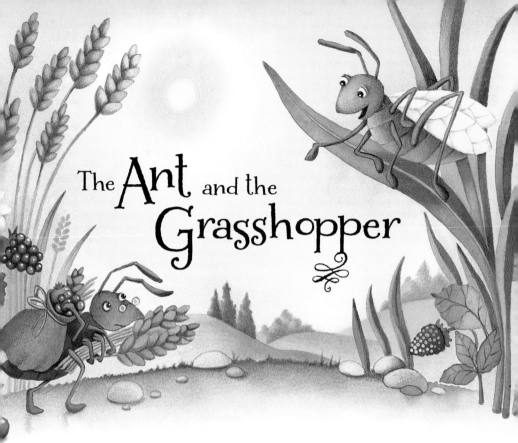

The Ant and the Grasshopper

The sun shone, the birds sang, bees buzzed and Ant... ran. He scurried this way and that, busy, busy, busy, on his little brown legs, never stopping for an instant. He scoured the fields looking for food — sheaves of wheat and barley which he carried over his back, nuts and berries stuffed to the brim of his small brown sack.

All through those long summer days, Ant worked, from the first light in the dawn skies to the fading sun at dusk.

"What are you doing?" asked Grasshopper, swaying giddily on the waving grass. He looked down at Ant, astonished. "I've watched you all day long," he remarked, "and you do nothing but work. Come on! Sit back, put your legs up, enjoy the sunshine while it lasts."

Ant shook his head and marched on. "No time to stop," he muttered. "No time to talk. I'm finding food for winter."

Grasshopper laughed,
leaped in the air and
fluttered down again.
"Chirrup, chirrup,
chirrup," he sang,
soaking up the
sunshine. "Winter
is months away. Poor
Ant," he pondered. "He just
doesn't know how to enjoy himself."

And so while Ant worked, Grasshopper
sang the summer away, his songs wafting on the
breeze. He often watched the little insect with
pity. Just once, Ant stopped in his tracks and
spoke to Grasshopper again.

"What will you do when winter comes?"
he asked. "There won't be any food for you
then, you know."

Grasshopper smiled. "Why should I worry
about winter now? I live for today," he boasted.
"You need to learn how to be happy and
carefree. You need to be more like me!"

"Just you wait," muttered Ant. "Just you wait
and see…"

It seemed as if summer would last forever.
The days were endless, bathed in light. The
earth breathed warmth, flowers bloomed and
food was everywhere. Grasshopper soon forgot
about the little ant and his funny ways.

But then slowly, slowly, all around him,

things began to change.

The days grew shorter, the nights grew
colder, and there was a chill nipping at the air.
The flowers bowed their heads, their petals fell
and scattered. The trees waved their branches
in the wind and tossed away their leaves.

Grasshopper stood on the bank and sang.
He tried to sing his carefree song of summer
but his notes hung in the air, long and
haunting. He wanted to hum with the bees,
who had buzzed from flower to flower, but they
had gone. He wanted to sing to the birds, to
the swifts and swallows who had danced and
soared above him all summer long, but they
too had flown, calling goodbye as they set off in

search of the sun.

And with each passing day, Grasshopper found less food to eat.

"What will I do," he began to wonder, "when winter comes?"

When it came, it came quickly. One morning he woke to find the ground hard with frost. Ice glittered and dazzled in the weak winter sun and the day seemed over when barely begun.

In the early dark, Grasshopper crawled over to a pile of leaves, shivering beneath his makeshift shelter. "I'll not last long," he thought. "I have no home to go to, no food to eat. I lived a careless summer."

He sniffed and sighed. "Poor me," he whispered. "Poor foolish Grasshopper." Then he shut his eyes, thinking to rest for a little while. But someone or something was tapping him, nudging him, trying to make him move.

"Grasshopper!" came a voice. "Wake up, wake up!"

Reluctantly, Grasshopper opened his eyes.
There was Ant, waving his little legs, frowning
at him furiously.

"You'd better come with me," he said.

Grasshopper dragged himself up and
followed Ant across the frozen ground. A light
snow was starting to fall; large white flakes,
bigger than Ant himself, drifted slowly down
from the overcast sky. Everything was quiet,
every sound muffled. Grasshopper wondered if
he were in a dream as he followed Ant under
the snow, down a hole, into the ground.

They went deeper and deeper into the
warm dry earth, and Grasshopper could see
tunnels stretching out in every direction,

twisting this way and that. He glimpsed little rooms bursting with food – seeds in one, nuts in another... "My store cupboards," said Ant, pride in his voice.

At last they came to the room at the very end of the tunnel. It was low and round with a warm bed of hay on the ground.

"I worked all summer," said Ant, "collecting food and bedding for winter. Now I am safe and snug."

Grasshopper hung his head. "If only I had done the same," he said.

Then, for the first time, Ant smiled at Grasshopper. "Stay with me this winter. You can share my food, live in my house, sleep in

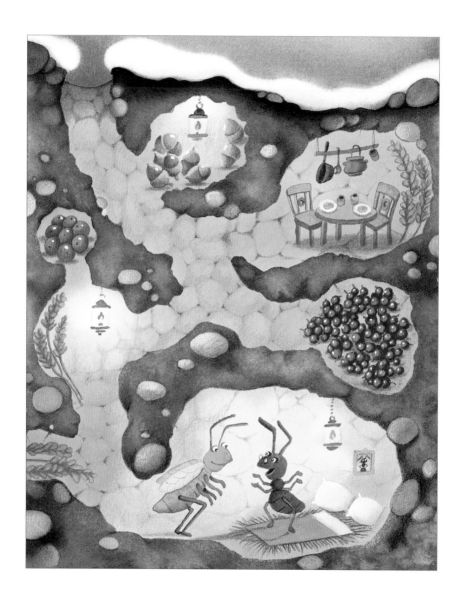

my warm, dry bed."

"Thank you!" cried Grasshopper. "Then next summer I'll do the same as you – work hard, find food. No more lazing around. No more chirruping in the breeze for me. I'm a changed insect!"

Ant laughed. "We'll see," was all he said.

Moral:
Beware of winter before it comes.

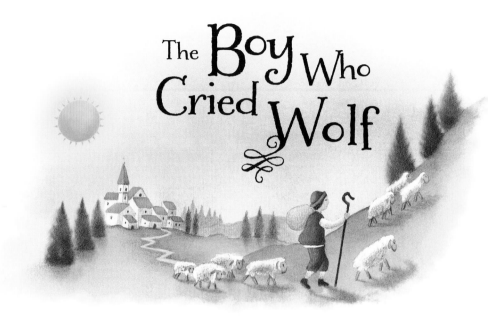

The Boy Who Cried Wolf

The boy herded the flock up the hillside, swinging his bag on his back and whistling to himself. Day after day he watched over the sheep on the hill, sometimes daydreaming, sometimes singing, always longing for the hustle and bustle of the city, rather than the lonely hills of his home.

But today was going to be different. He had a brilliant trick in mind. No more boredom for him! He was going to make today exciting...

The boy waited until he reached the very top of the hill, standing on a rock above the grazing sheep. Then he opened his mouth and shouted as loud as he could, "Wolf! Help! There's a wolf on the hill." And he pulled his horn from his bag and blew on it.

The villagers heard his cries. "A wolf?" they gulped. "Run! Run for the hills! We must save our sheep."

They came puffing and pounding up the

hill, old men and boys, young girls and wives, waving sticks and brooms, rakes and rolling pins – anything they could find.

When they reached the top, they looked around. "Where's the wolf?" they cried.

The boy laughed and laughed. "There is no wolf," he replied. "I tricked you! Hee hee hee. I tricked you all. You looked so funny, panting up the hill..." He broke off to laugh some more.

The villagers were not happy.

"Don't do that again," the men scolded.

"Bad boy!" said the women, wagging their fingers at him.

And they stomped, one and all, back down

the hill.

The boy waited until they were right at the very bottom. Then, with a sly smile, he climbed on his rock again and shouted. "Help! Wolf! There really *is* a wolf this time. Please come!" And he blew even louder and harder on his horn.

The villagers heard the urgency in his voice. "There really must be a wolf this time..." they said to each other.

Once again they turned and ran up the hill, puffing and panting till they reached the top.

The boy laughed and laughed until tears ran down his face. "I did it again!" he cried, jumping up and down. "I tricked you! I tricked you."

"We'll not believe you a third time," said the villagers, before they took off for home. But the boy was too busy congratulating himself to listen.

He had just settled back against a tree, an apple in his hand, when he heard a stealthy pad, pad, padding noise on the soft earth, and the sound of twigs snapping underfoot. He looked up to see a large black wolf creeping out from behind a bush. He jumped up with a start.

"A wolf," he whispered to himself. "A real wolf."

With trembling hands, he reached for his horn and blew on it as hard as he could.

"Wolf! Wolf!" he cried, again and again. But no one came. His voice was soon hoarse from shouting, but no villagers appeared on the brow of the hill.

The boy could only watch in horror as the wolf devoured some sheep and scattered the rest across the hills.

As night fell, the boy slunk back down the hill, bringing no sheep behind him.

"Where's our flock? What have you done with our sheep?" demanded the villagers.

"A wolf came," sobbed the boy. "I called for you. Why didn't you come?"

"How could we know you were telling the truth?" the villagers replied. "You had tricked us twice before."

The boy hung his head in shame. "I'll never cry wolf again," he said.

Moral:
No one believes a liar,
even when he tells the truth.

Zeus and the Tortoise

It was Zeus's wedding feast. Every creature under the sun had been invited. The tables groaned with food – loaves of crusty bread, plates piled high with shiny~scaled fish, bowls bursting with bunches of grapes and rosy ripe peaches and pears. Zeus looked around with great satisfaction until he realized, with a start, that someone was missing.

"Tortoise!" he boomed. "Where is Tortoise?"

A hush fell over the table. At once the chatter and laughter stopped. Everyone was afraid of Zeus and his fiery temper.

At last, a mouse summoned up the courage to speak. "He stayed at home," she squeaked.

Zeus turned puce with anger. He thumped the table with his fist, cracking it in two. "How dare Tortoise not come to my wedding feast!" he stormed.

The animals watched and waited to see what would happen next, but Zeus only picked up his glass and drank from it.

"Perhaps he'll forget about it?" said the birds on the way home.

"Do you think we should warn Tortoise?" wondered the bears.

"No," the animals decided together. "There's nothing Tortoise can do now."

The very next day, Tortoise was sitting in his little cave, happily munching on some old green leaves.

"Is this what you prefer to my feast?" came a voice like thunder.

Tortoise looked up to see Zeus standing before him, filling the entrance to his cave, blocking out the sunlight. His face was filled with fury.

"It is," Tortoise replied calmly. "There's no place like home."

"In that case," Zeus retorted, dangerously quiet now, "you can carry your home on your back for the rest of your days."

Zeus raised the staff in his hand and fired a thunderbolt. Tortoise felt something hard and heavy strike his back... and stay there. He turned around, craning his neck to see what it could be, and gasped at the huge domed shell that covered him. He shook himself one way, then another, but it wouldn't budge.

"Ha!" said Zeus, and left.

Tortoise crawled forward. The thing was so heavy he could barely walk, just shuffle forward on splayed legs. The other animals gathered around him, looking on with a mixture of pity and horror.

"Is this what he did to you?" asked Bear.

Tortoise slowly nodded.

"Well," said Rabbit, not unkindly, "at least you'll always have a home. Maybe you should try it out. Can you fit inside it?"

Tortoise tried. He drew back his head, he drew in his legs, until he was safe and snug inside. It felt dark and warm in his shell, like his very own, perfectly~shaped cave.

When Tortoise next poked his head out, he was beaming.

"Ah," he sighed. "If Zeus meant this as a punishment, he made a mistake. Home, sweet home," he added, and snuggled back inside.

Moral:
There's no place like home.

About the stories

All of the stories in this book were first told long, long ago – in fact, so long ago that no one actually knows *who* told them. They may have been written by a man called Aesop who lived in Greece over two thousand years ago.

One ancient tale about Aesop says he was a

very ugly slave who was so clever he gained his freedom and went to work for a king. Another story says he met a grisly end: thrown off a cliff to his death.

The stories themselves are 'fables', which means they have a moral, or a lesson, at the end. They are mostly about animals, though some are about plants or objects, which all speak and act like humans.

In Ancient Greece, students would learn fables, retell them and even make up new ones as a way to win arguments. You can still use fables like this today. Why not try inventing your own...

Acknowledgements

Designed by Nancy Leschnikoff and Katie Lovell
Additional design by Sam Chandler
Edited by Lesley Sims
Digital manipulation by Nick Wakeford

First published in 2013 by Usborne Publishing Ltd., 83-85 Saffron Hill, London EC1N 8RT, England. www.usborne.com
Copyright © 2013 Usborne Publishing Limited.